Babar and the Doctor

LAURENT DE BRUNHOFF

BABAR

AND THE DOCTOR

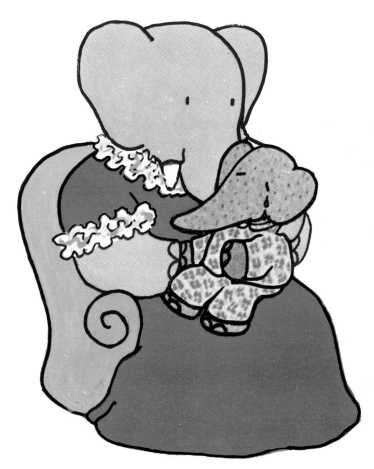

LITTLE
MAMMOTH

Babar and Celeste were having a meal
with their children, Pom, Flora and Alexander.
But the children were not a bit hungry.
For pudding there was a beautiful cake.

It was pineapple cream shortcake,
iced, and decorated with slices of orange
and pretty crystallised cherries.
The children didn't want any of it—
although usually they were rather greedy!
"What's the matter?" asked Celeste anxiously.
"Are you feeling ill?"

Babar quickly telephoned the doctor.
'Is that Dr Capoulosse? This is Babar.
Pom, Flora and Alexander are ill.
They haven't any appetite
even for their pudding.
Can you come and see them?"

Meanwhile Celeste helped the children
to put on their pyjamas ready for bed.
They were all miserable and tearful.
Celeste felt their foreheads and trunks.
They were hot. They all had temperatures
and Flora complained of a sore throat.

The doorbell rang. Babar himself
went to open it. It was the doctor.
"My dear Capoulosse," said Babar,
"how good of you to come so quickly.
Celeste and I are worried."

The doctor peered down the children's throats
with the help of his torch.

Then he listened to their breathing
with his stethoscope.
"Cough!" he ordered them.
"Again . . . Good. It's measles."
"That's just what I thought!"
said the Old Lady.

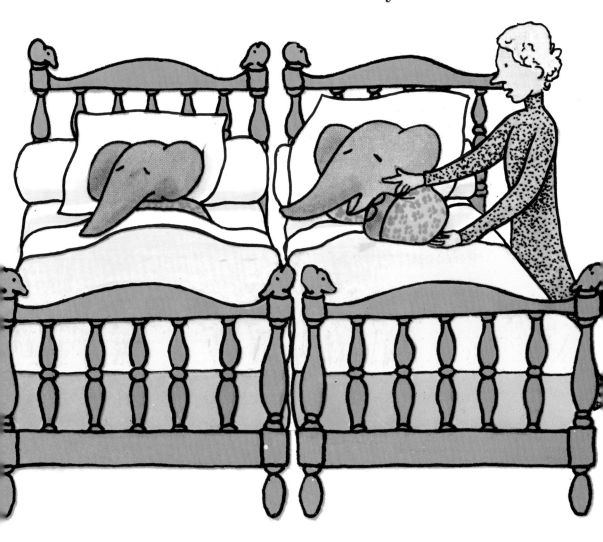

Next day Pom, Flora and Alexander
were covered in spots.
Celeste and the Old Lady looked after them
and took their temperatures night and morning.

The children did not like
their medicine very much.
But they had to do
what the doctor ordered.

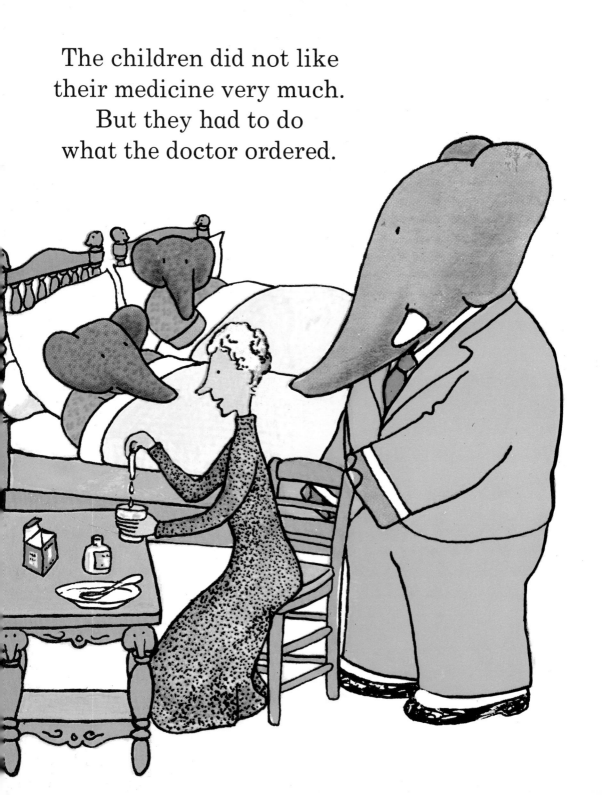

At night they were feverish.
They slept badly. Celeste often
went softly in to see if they needed her.
Alexander tossed about so much
that he fell out of bed! Celeste
held him in her arms to comfort him.

Measles isn't a serious illness,
so after a few days the children
were able to get up. But they stayed
in their room and played quiet games.

Babar brought them presents.
He gave Pom and Alexander
two marvellous racing cars.
Flora had a toy clown
which made a noise
when it was squeezed.

Soon the children felt perfectly well.
They had had enough of keeping quiet,
so when their friends
Arthur and Zephir came to see them
they attacked them with pillows!

What a fight it was! Arthur and Pom
were in a snowstorm of feathers,
and laughed till they had no breath left.
Zephir turned somersaults
and played with Flora and Alexander.

They were completely cured.
Dr Capoulosse
let them go out
for the first time.

Pom, Flora and Alexander went into the garden
with Babar, Celeste and Dr Capoulosse.
Flora insisted on taking her doll with her,
and was very pleased
when Poutifour, the gardener,
gave the doll a grape.

Next day . . . Poor Arthur!
Poor Zephir! They weren't at all well.
They had caught the measles too!
Fortunately Celeste
knew exactly how to take care of them.

First published in Great Britain 1972
by Methuen Children's Books Ltd
Magnet paperback edition first published 1982
First published 1969 by Librairie Hachette, Paris, as *Babar et le docteur*
Reissued 1991 by Little Mammoth
an imprint of Mandarin Paperbacks
Michelin House, 81 Fulham Road, London SW3 6RB

Reprinted 1991

Mandarin is an imprint of the Octopus Publishing Group